The Adventures of
Pinocchio

The Adventures of

Pinocchio

C. COLLODI

Condensed and adapted by
W.T. Robinson

From a translation by
Carol Dessa Chiesa

Illustrated by
Alastair Graham

Cover illustrated by
Ritva Voutila

Dalmatian Press

The Dalmatian Press Great Classics for Children
have been adapted and illustrated with care and thought
to introduce you to a world of famous authors, characters, ideas,
and great stories that have been loved for generations.

Editor — Kathryn Knight
Creative Director — Gina Rhodes-Haynes
And the entire classics project team of Dalmatian Press

THE ADVENTURES OF PINOCCHIO
Copyright © 2009 Dalmatian Press, LLC

RL: 3.4

The DALMATIAN PRESS name is a trademark of Dalmatian Press, LLC,
Franklin, Tennessee 37067 • 1-866-418-2572

ISBN: 1-40375-798-4
17323C

09 10   11 12 NG 33648 10 9 8 7 6 5 4 3 2 1

A note to the reader—

A classic story rests in your hands. The characters are famous. The tale is timeless.

This Great Classic for Children by Dalmatian Press has been carefully condensed and adapted from the original version (which you really *must* read when you're ready for every detail). We kept the well-known phrases for you. We kept the author's style. And we kept the important imagery and heart of the tale.

Literature is terrific fun! It encourages you to think. It helps you dream. It is full of heroes and villains, suspense and humor, adventure and wonder, and new ideas. It introduces you to writers who reach out across time to say: "Do you want to hear a story I wrote?"

Curl up and enjoy.

DALMATIAN PRESS
GREAT CLASSICS FOR CHILDREN

ALICE'S ADVENTURES IN WONDERLAND

ANNE OF GREEN GABLES

BLACK BEAUTY

THE CALL OF THE WILD

THE STORY OF DOCTOR DOLITTLE

FRANKENSTEIN

DR. JEKYLL AND MR. HYDE

HUCKLEBERRY FINN

THE LEGEND OF SLEEPY HOLLOW
RIP VAN WINKLE
THE SPECTRE BRIDEGROOM

A LITTLE PRINCESS

LITTLE WOMEN

MOBY DICK

PETER PAN

PINOCCHIO

THE SECRET GARDEN

THE TIME MACHINE

TOM SAWYER

TREASURE ISLAND

THE WIND IN THE WILLOWS

THE WONDERFUL WIZARD OF OZ

CONTENTS

CHARACTERS

PINOCCHIO OR PUPPET — a foolish, impulsive puppet who must learn how to work

MASTRO ANTONIO — a carpenter who gives away a talking piece of wood

GEPPETTO OR FATHER — the loving wood-carver, Pinocchio's father

TALKING CRICKET — a wise creature, he tries to give Pinocchio good advice

HARLEQUIN AND PULCINELLA — puppets who welcome Pinocchio to the Puppet Theater

FIRE EATER — the Puppet Master

FOX AND CAT — two false friends trying to trick Pinocchio

FAIRY WITH BLUE HAIR — the kind, motherly Fairy who looks after Pinocchio

CROW AND OWL — with the Talking Cricket, the doctors the Fairy calls to take care of Pinocchio

CHARACTERS

GORILLA JUDGE — puts Pinocchio in prison for being a fool

TERRIBLE WHALE — swallows Geppetto

TEACHER — encourages Pinocchio to study

EUGENE — one of Pinocchio's schoolmates

GREEN FISHERMAN — catches Pinocchio in his net

LAMPWICK — the most mischievous boy in Pinocchio's school

CIRCUS OWNER — teaches his new donkey, Pinocchio, to dance

FARMER GIANGIO — gives Pinocchio honest work to do

BLACKBIRD, FALCON, MEDORO, CRAB, PARROT, PIGEON, DOLPHIN, ALIDORO, SNAIL, DORMOUSE, AND TUNA — all creatures who give Pinocchio help or good advice

CHAPTER ONE

A Lively Puppet of Oak

A long time ago, in Italy, there once was—

What do you think, dear readers? A king, you say? A prince? No, my children, you are wrong. Once there was a piece of wood—just a plain oak log lying in the corner of a carpenter's shop.

The carpenter's name was Mastro Antonio. But everyone called him Mastro Cherry, for the tip of his nose was so round and red and shiny that it looked like a ripe cherry.

One fine day, Mastro Cherry spied that piece of wood and was filled with joy. "This has come just in time," he thought. "I shall use it to make the leg of a table."

But just as he picked up his hatchet and began, he heard a wee little voice whine, "Please be careful! Do not hit me so hard!"

Mastro Cherry looked around with frightened eyes to see where that little voice had come from. He saw no one!

"Oh, I see!" he said, laughing and scratching his wig. "I only *thought* I heard that tiny voice! Well, well—back to work."

"Oh, oh! You hurt!" cried the same small voice.

Mastro Cherry's eyes grew larger and his mouth opened wide. "Where did that voice come from, when there is no one around? Has this piece of wood learned to cry like a child? Or—could someone be hidden in it? If so, I'll fix him!"

With these words, he grabbed the log with both hands and threw it to the floor. Hearing nothing, he picked up the shaving knife and began smoothing the wood. But as he drew the blade back and forth, he heard the tiny voice giggle, "Stop it! Oh, stop it! Ha, ha, ha! You tickle my stomach!"

Poor Mastro Cherry fainted. When he opened his eyes, he was sitting on the floor and someone was knocking on his door.

"Come in," called the carpenter, for he hadn't the strength to stand up. The door opened and in came a well-dressed little old man named Geppetto.

"Good day, Mastro Cherry," said Geppetto. "What are you doing on the floor?"

"I am teaching the ants their A-B-Cs. And what brought you here, friend Geppetto?"

"My legs. *And* I have come to ask a favor."

"Here I am. How can I help you?"

"I want to make myself a beautiful wooden puppet—one that will be able to dance and turn somersaults. Then I'll take it around the world and earn some money."

"Well, then, Mastro Geppetto," said the carpenter, "what is it you want from me?"

"Would you give me a piece of wood to make this puppet?"

Mastro Antonio knew *exactly* which piece of wood he would gladly give away. He picked up the "talking" log that had scared him so. As he held it out to his friend, it somehow jumped out of his hands and hit against poor Geppetto's thin legs.

"Ah! Is this the kind way, Mastro Cherry, in which you make your gifts? You have made me almost lame!" cried Geppetto.

"I swear to you I did not do it! It's the fault of this piece of wood," said Mastro Cherry.

"Well, I don't see how. It must be a strange piece of wood!"

"In some ways it is… But never mind. Take it and I wish you luck with it."

Geppetto thanked him and limped away.

As soon as he reached home, Geppetto took his tools and began to shape the wood into a puppet.

"What shall I call him?" he said to himself. "I think I'll call him PINOCCHIO. This name will make him famous. I once knew a family with that name, and they were all lucky and happy."

After choosing a name, Geppetto began to make the hair, the head, and the eyes. Imagine his surprise when he noticed that these eyes moved and then stared right at him!

"Ugly wooden eyes, why do you stare at me?" Geppetto cried.

There was no answer.

After the eyes, Geppetto made the nose, and—guess what! That nose began to grow longer! It stretched and stretched—longer and longer! The more he cut, the longer it grew. He finally gave up on it to begin on the mouth.

As soon as the mouth was finished, it began to laugh at him.

"Stop laughing! Stop laughing, I say!" roared Geppetto.

The mouth stopped laughing, but it stuck out a long tongue. Geppetto made believe he saw nothing and went on, making the chin, the neck, the body, the arms, and the hands.

As he was finishing the fingers, Geppetto felt his wig being pulled off. And what did he see? His yellow wig was in the puppet's hand.

"Pinocchio, give me my wig!"

But instead of giving it back, Pinocchio put it on his own head. At that naughty trick, Geppetto became even more upset.

"Pinocchio, you wicked boy! You are not yet finished, and already you are playing tricks on your poor old father. Very bad, my son!"

The legs and feet still had to be made. As soon as they were done, Geppetto felt a sharp kick on the tip of his nose. He was so mad that he wanted to spank Pinocchio. But, holding his temper, he put the Puppet on the floor and began teaching him to walk.

As his legs loosened up, Pinocchio started running around the room. He came to the open door, and with one leap he was flying down the street! Poor Geppetto ran after him but could not catch him, for Pinocchio ran like the wind.

"Catch him! Catch him!" Geppetto kept shouting. But the people, seeing a wooden puppet running in the street, only laughed till they cried.

Luckily, a policeman came along and stood in the middle of the street, with legs wide apart. Pinocchio tried his best to escape between the legs of the big fellow, but the policeman grabbed him by his long nose and returned him to Mastro Geppetto. The old man held Pinocchio by the back of the neck and shook him two or three times.

"We're going home now," Geppetto shouted. "When we get home, I'll give you a good spanking!"

Hearing this, Pinocchio threw himself on the ground and would not take another step.

"Poor Puppet," called out a man. "I am not surprised he doesn't want to go home. Geppetto will probably beat him. If we leave that poor Puppet in his hands, he may tear him to pieces!"

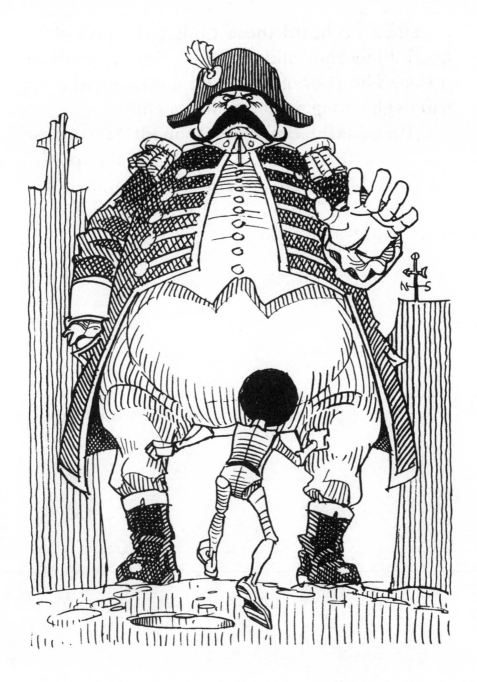

When he heard these things, the policeman freed Pinocchio and dragged Geppetto off to prison. The poor old man did not know what he had done wrong and cried like a child.

"Unthankful boy!" he sobbed. "I tried so hard to make you a nice, well-behaved puppet!"

What happened after this is a strange and exciting story. You may read it, dear children, in the chapters that follow.

CHAPTER TWO

Advice from a Cricket

As soon as Pinocchio was set free, he ran wildly through the fields toward home, like a rabbit chased by hounds. When he got to the house, he slipped inside and locked the door, happy to be safe. But his happiness lasted only a short time, for just then he heard someone saying:

"Cri-cri-cri!"

"Who is calling me?" asked Pinocchio, very frightened.

"I am!"

Pinocchio turned and saw a large Cricket crawling up the wall.

"Tell me, Cricket, who are you?"

"I am the Talking Cricket. I have been living in this room for more than one hundred years."

"Today this room is mine," said the Puppet, "and you may just get out right now!"

"I refuse to leave this spot," answered the Cricket, "until I have told you a great truth."

"Tell it, then, and hurry."

"Sad things happen to boys who disobey their parents and run away from home!" said the Cricket. "They will never be happy in this world."

"Sing on, my dear Cricket, if you wish. But tomorrow morning I leave this place forever. If I stay here, I'll have to go to school and study. Let me tell you, I hate to study! It's much more fun to chase butterflies, climb trees, and steal bird nests."

"Poor silly thing!" said the Cricket. "Don't you know that if you go on like that, you will be as dumb as a donkey?"

"Keep still, you ugly Cricket!" cried Pinocchio.

But the Cricket, who was a wise old thinker, said, "If you do not like going to school, why don't you at least learn a skill, so that you can get a job and earn an honest living?"

"The only skills *I* like are eating, sleeping, and playing from morning till night!" said the Puppet.

"Let me tell you something for your own good, Pinocchio," said the Talking Cricket in his calm voice. "Those who follow *that* line of work always end up in trouble."

"Careful, Cricket! If you make me angry, you'll be sorry!"

"Poor Pinocchio, I *am* sorry—for *you*."

"Why?"

"Because you are a Puppet with a hard, wooden head with hard, unkind thoughts."

At these last words, Pinocchio jumped up in anger and threw a hammer at the Talking Cricket. Sad to say, my dear children, he hit the Cricket square on its head. With a weak "cri-cri-cri," the poor Cricket fell from the wall—dead!

Pinocchio didn't spend any time thinking about the poor Cricket, for his stomach was empty. He searched all around the room—even under the bed—for a scrap of food. He found nothing. Night was coming and he was dizzy and faint from hunger.

"The Talking Cricket was right," he moaned. "I was wrong to disobey Father and run away from home. If he were here now, I wouldn't be so hungry! Oh, how horrible it is to be hungry!"

He decided to walk to the nearby village, hoping to find some kind person who might give him a bit of bread.

The night was black. Thunder rumbled and lightning flashed. An angry, cold wind shook the trees, making them whistle in a scary way.

Pinocchio ran on with leaps and bounds, his tongue hanging out. When he got to the village, it was as dark and lonely as a ghost town. Not even a dog barked. Pinocchio ran up to a door and knocked wildly. An old man in a nightcap opened an upstairs window and looked out.

"What do you want at this time of night?" the man called angrily.

"Will you be good enough to give me a bit of bread? I am hungry."

"Wait a minute! I'll come right back," called the old fellow. (He knew *just* what to give rascals who woke people in the middle of the night.)

Suddenly, Pinocchio felt a shower of ice-cold water crash down on his wooden head. The old man laughed from the open window.

Soaking wet and tired from hunger, Pinocchio went home. He sat down on a little stool, put his feet on the stove to dry them, and fell asleep.

While Pinocchio snored away, his wooden feet caught fire and burned to ashes. At dawn, a loud knocking at the door awakened him.

"Who is it?" he called, yawning and rubbing his eyes.

"It is I," answered the voice of Geppetto.

The poor Puppet was still half-asleep and did not know that his feet were burned and gone. When he heard his father's voice, he jumped up to open the door—and fell clattering to the floor like a sack of wood.

"Open the door for me!" Geppetto shouted.

"Father, dear Father, I can't," answered the crying Puppet. "Something has eaten my feet!"

Geppetto, thinking this was just another of the Puppet's tricks, climbed in through the window.

At first he was very angry. But when he saw that Pinocchio really had no feet, he became very sad. He picked him up and held him close, while the tears ran down his cheeks.

"My little Pinocchio, my dear little Pinocchio! How did you burn your feet?"

"I don't know, Father, but I have had a terrible night, and I'm starving!"

Geppetto listened to Pinocchio's sad story. Then he pulled three pears out of his pocket.

"These three pears were for my breakfast," he said, "but I give them to you gladly. Eat them and stop crying."

"If you want me to eat them, please peel them for me," said Pinocchio.

"Peel them?" asked Geppetto, very much surprised. "You must not be so fussy about your food, dear boy. In this world, even as children, we must learn to eat all sorts of foods, for we never know where our next meal may come from!"

"You may be right," answered Pinocchio, "but I will not eat the pears if they are not peeled. I don't like them."

Kind old Geppetto took out a knife and peeled the skins from the pears.

Pinocchio ate the pears in a flash and started to throw the cores and skins away, but Geppetto held his arm.

"Oh, no, don't throw those away! Everything in this world may be of some use!"

"I will not eat them!" snapped Pinocchio.

"You might change your mind," said the kind old Geppetto quietly.

Geppetto was right, for soon Pinocchio began whining and crying that he was still hungry.

"But I have no more to give you," said Geppetto.

"Really? Nothing—nothing?"

"I have only three cores and these skins."

"Very well, then," said Pinocchio, "I'll eat them."

At first he made a bad face and turned up his nose. But, one after another, the skins and the cores disappeared.

"Ah! Now I feel fine!" he said, after eating the last skin.

"You see," said Geppetto, "I was right when I told you that we must not be too fussy about food. My dear, we never know what tomorrow may bring."

CHAPTER THREE

New Feet and Clothes

Just as soon as his stomach was full, Pinocchio started to grumble and cry to Geppetto that he wanted a new pair of feet.

"Why should I give you feet? You will just run away from home again."

"I promise you," sobbed the Puppet, "that from now on I'll be good—"

"Boys always promise that, when they want something," said Geppetto.

"I promise to go to school every day, to study, and to work and—"

"Boys always sing that song, when they want their own way."

"But I am better than other boys, and I always tell the truth. I promise you, Father, that I'll find a job and take care of you in your old age."

Geppetto's eyes filled with tears and his heart softened. In less than an hour, the feet were finished and glued to Pinocchio's ankles.

As soon as the Puppet felt his new feet, he skipped with joy and cried, "Oh, thank you, Father! Now I'll go to school! But I'll need some clothes."

Geppetto did not have a penny in his pocket, so he made his son a little suit of flowered paper, a pair of shoes from the bark of a tree, and a tiny cap from a bit of dough.

"Now I look like a gentleman!" Pinocchio shouted proudly. "But I still need something else for school."

"What is it?"

"An A-B-C book."

"You are right! But how shall we get it?"

"That's easy. You can go to a store and buy it."

"But I have no money," said the old man sadly.

Pinocchio looked so unhappy at these words, that Geppetto cried, "Oh, well, what does it matter, after all?" And, putting on his old, ragged coat, he ran out of the house.

When he returned he had the A-B-C book for his son, but the old coat was gone. The poor fellow was in his shirtsleeves.

"It is cold outside. Where's your coat, Father?"

"I have sold it."

"Why did you sell your coat?"

"It was too warm," Geppetto fibbed.

Pinocchio knew the truth, and could not hold back his tears. He hugged his father and kissed him over and over. Then Pinocchio hurried off to school with his new A-B-C book under his arm.

"In school today," he thought, "I'll learn to read, tomorrow to write, and the day after tomorrow I'll do arithmetic. Then I can earn a lot of money. With the very first pennies I make, I'll buy Father a new coat made of gold and silver with diamond buttons. That poor man sold his only coat on this cold day to buy a book for me. Fathers are so good to their children!"

As he neared a village, he thought he heard sounds of horns and drums coming from a side street—*Too-too-toot, too-too-toot… boom, boom, boom, boom.*

"Oh! Someone is having fun! What a pain that I have to go to school! Otherwise…"

There he stopped, wondering what to do. Should he go to school, or follow the horns?

"Today I'll follow the horns, and tomorrow I'll go to school," he thought.

And he forgot all about his promises to his father and to himself.

CHAPTER FOUR

The Puppet Theater

He ran down the street like the wind. The sounds of horn and drum grew louder—*Too-too-toot, too-too-toot… boom, boom, boom, boom!*

Suddenly he came to a large town square. The square was full of people standing in front of a brightly painted building.

"What is that house?" Pinocchio asked a boy.

"Read the sign and you'll know."

"I'd like to read, but… somehow I can't today."

"Oh, really? Then I'll read it to you. It says: GREAT PUPPET THEATER."

"And how much does it cost to get in?"

"Four pennies."

Pinocchio, who was wild to know what was going on inside, begged the boy to loan him four pennies. When that didn't work, he offered to sell his coat, then his shoes, and finally his hat.

The boy just laughed and made jokes about his paper coat, wooden shoes, and dough cap.

Pinocchio was almost in tears. Then he had another idea... but he wasn't sure... Oh, he could not make up his mind... At last he said, "Will you give me four pennies for the book?"

"I am a boy and I buy nothing from boys," said the little fellow.

"*I'll* give you four pennies for your A-B-C book," said a rag-picker who stood close by.

Then and there, the book was sold. Just think! Poor old Geppetto sat at home shivering with cold because he had sold his only coat to buy that little book for his son!

Quick as a flash, Pinocchio took the four pennies, paid at the window, and ran into the Puppet Theater. Two puppets were on the stage—one named Harlequin, the other Pulcinella. They were teasing and playing tricks on each other, as puppets do in puppet shows.

Suddenly, Harlequin stopped talking, pointed toward the audience, and yelled, "Look, look! Am I dreaming? Or do I really see Pinocchio there?"

"Yes, yes! It is Pinocchio!" screamed Pulcinella.

"It is Pinocchio! It is Pinocchio!" cried all the puppets, running out from behind the stage. "Hurrah for Pinocchio!"

"Pinocchio, come up here!" shouted Harlequin. "Come to the arms of your wooden brothers!"

At such loving words, Pinocchio leaped to the stage. The puppets greeted him with screams of joy, knocking together in warm, wooden puppet hugs. But the audience, seeing that the play had stopped, became angry.

"The play! The play! We want the play!" they all yelled.

The yelling did no good. Instead of going on with their act, the puppets lifted Pinocchio to their shoulders and carried him around the stage.

At that very moment, the Puppet Master came out of his room. What a horrible looking man! His beard was as black as coal, and so long that it reached from his chin down to his feet. His mouth was as wide as an oven, his teeth like yellow fangs, and his eyes like two glowing red coals.

In his huge, hairy hands he held a whip made of green snakes and black cat tails twisted together.

"Why have you caused this trouble in my theater?" the huge man asked Pinocchio, in a deep, dark voice.

"Believe me, sir, it was not my fault," croaked Pinocchio.

"Enough! Be quiet! I'll take care of you later."

As soon as the play was over, the Puppet Master hung poor Pinocchio up on a nail. Then he went to the kitchen, where a fine lamb was roasting in the oven. He called Harlequin and Pulcinella and said to them, "Bring that puppet to me! He looks as if he is made of good, dry wood. He'll make a fine roasting fire."

A few minutes later, Pinocchio was carried in, crying and squirming like an eel.

"Father, save me! I don't want to die! I don't want to die!"

Fire Eater (this was the Puppet Master's name) was ugly, but he wasn't as bad as he looked. When he saw Pinocchio struggling with fear and crying, he began to feel sorry for him. Finally, he could control himself no longer and gave a loud sneeze.

"Good news, brother of mine!" whispered Harlequin to Pinocchio. "Fire Eater has sneezed, and this is a sign that he feels sorry for you. When he is sad, instead of crying, he sneezes. You are saved!"

"Stop crying!" said Fire Eater. "It gives me a funny feeling and—Ahh–*tchoo! Ahh–tchoo!*"

"God bless you!" said Pinocchio.

"Thanks! Are your father and mother still living?" asked Fire Eater.

"My father, yes. My mother I've never known."

"Your poor father would suffer terribly if I were to use you as firewood. Poor old man! I feel sorry for him! Ahh—tchoo! *Ahh—tchoo!*"

"God bless you!" said Pinocchio.

"Thanks! However, I ought to be sorry for myself, too. My good dinner is spoiled. I have no more wood for the fire, and the lamb is only half-cooked. Never mind! In your place I'll burn some other puppet. Hey, there! Officers!"

At the call, two wooden officers appeared, long and thin as pieces of rope, with odd-looking hats on their heads and swords in their hands.

"Take Harlequin and throw him on the fire," ordered Fire Eater. "I want my lamb well cooked!"

Think how poor Harlequin felt! He was so scared that his legs doubled up under him and he fell to the floor.

Pinocchio threw himself at the feet of Fire Eater. Weeping bitterly, he begged in a sad, quiet voice, "Have pity, kind sir!"

"Well, what do you want now, Puppet?"

"I beg for mercy for my poor friend Harlequin. He has never done any harm in his life."

"There is no mercy here, Pinocchio. I have let you go. Harlequin must burn in your place."

"In that case," announced Pinocchio, "I see what I must do. Come, officers! Throw me on the flames. It is not fair for Harlequin to die in my place!"

These brave words made all the other puppets cry—even the wooden officers. Fire Eater at first stayed hard and cold as a piece of ice. But then, little by little, he softened and began to sneeze. And after four or five sneezes, he opened his arms to Pinocchio.

"You are a brave boy!" he said. "Come to my arms and kiss me!"

Pinocchio ran to him and, scurrying like a squirrel up the long black beard, he gave Fire Eater a loving kiss on the tip of his nose.

"And you're not going to burn me?" asked Harlequin.

"No, you are saved," answered Fire Eater. "Tonight I shall eat my lamb only half-cooked."

At the news that Harlequin was safe, the puppets ran to the stage where they laughed and danced all night.

The next morning, Fire Eater had some questions for Pinocchio.

"What is your father's name?" he asked.

"Geppetto."

"And what is his work?"

"He's a woodcarver."

"Does he earn much?"

"He never has an extra penny. He had to sell his only coat just to buy me an A-B-C book."

"Poor man! Here. Take these five gold coins, before I start sneezing. Go—give them to him."

Pinocchio thanked him a thousand times and, filled with joy, left to go home.

CHAPTER FIVE

A Lame Fox and a Blind Cat

Pinocchio had gone only half a mile when he met a lame Fox and a blind Cat. The lame Fox leaned on the Cat, and the blind Cat let the Fox lead him along.

"Good day, Pinocchio," said the Fox politely.

"How do you know my name?" asked the little wooden Puppet.

"I know your father well. I saw him yesterday standing at the door of his house."

"And what was he doing?"

"He was in his shirt, shivering with cold."

"My poor father! But after today, he will suffer no longer."

"Why?"

"Because I have become a rich man."

"You, a rich man?" said the Fox, and he began to laugh out loud. The Cat was laughing also, but tried to hide it by stroking his long whiskers.

"There is nothing to laugh at," cried Pinocchio angrily. He pulled out the five gold coins that Fire Eater had given him.

At the cheerful jingle of the gold, the Fox, without thinking, held out his paw that was supposed to be lame, and the Cat opened wide his two eyes that were supposed to be blind, but he closed them again so quickly that Pinocchio did not notice.

"And what," asked the Fox, "are you going to do with all that money?"

"First of all," answered Pinocchio, "I want to buy a fine new coat for my father. A coat of gold and silver with diamond buttons! After that, I'll buy an A-B-C book, for I want to go to school and study hard."

"Look at me," said the Fox. "For the silly reason of wanting to study, I have a bad paw."

"Look at me," said the Cat. "For the same foolish reason, I have lost the sight of both eyes."

At that moment, a Blackbird, perched on a fence, called out, "Pinocchio, do not listen to bad advice. If you do, you'll be sorry!"

Poor little Blackbird! Quick as a wink, the Cat leaped on him and ate him, feathers and all. Then he cleaned his whiskers, closed his eyes, and became "blind" once more.

"Poor Blackbird!" said Pinocchio to the Cat. "Why did you kill him?"

"I killed him to teach him a lesson. He talks too much. Next time he'll know better."

After the three had walked for a while longer, the Fox turned to the Puppet and asked, "Do you want thousands more gold coins in place of the five you have?"

"Yes, but how?"

"Very easily. Don't go home. Come with us."

"And where will you take me?"

"To the City of Foolafool."

"No—no, I don't want to go," said Pinocchio, after thinking about it. "I'm going home where Father is waiting for me. I have been a bad son. The Talking Cricket was right when he said that a boy who does not obey his parents cannot be happy in this world."

"Well, then," said the Fox, "if you really want to go home, go ahead. But you'll be sorry."

"You'll be sorry," repeated the Cat.

"Think about it, Pinocchio. You are turning your back on the Fortune of a Lifetime."

"The Fortune of a Lifetime," repeated the Cat.

"But how can my coins possibly become so many more?" asked Pinocchio wonderingly.

"I'll explain," said the Fox. "Just outside the City of Foolafool, there is a magic place—the Field of Wonders! In this field you dig a hole, and you bury a gold coin. You water it well and go to bed. The next morning you find a beautiful vine loaded with five hundred gold coins."

"So that if I were to bury my five gold coins," cried Pinocchio with growing wonder, "then the next morning I should find—how many?"

"Twenty-five hundred!" answered the Fox.

"Oh, my!" cried Pinocchio, dancing with joy. "I shall keep two thousand for myself, and the other five hundred I'll give to you two."

"A gift for us?" cried the Fox, pretending to be upset. "Why, of course not! We do not work for profit. We work only to help others."

"To help others!" repeated the Cat.

"What good people! I'm with you. Let's go!" said Pinocchio, forgetting his father and all his good promises to himself.

Do you think, dear children, that Pinocchio has done the right thing? Keep reading, and you shall see.

CHAPTER SIX

An Attack by Bandits

Cat and Fox and Puppet walked and walked. That evening, they came to the *Red Lobster Inn*.

"Let us stop here," said the Fox, "to eat and rest a few hours. At midnight we'll start out again, for at dawn we must be at the Field of Wonders."

After supper, the Fox said to the innkeeper, "Give us two good rooms—one for Mr. Pinocchio, and the other for me and my friend. Before starting out, we'll take a little nap. Remember to call us at midnight, for we must be on our way."

"Yes, sir," answered the innkeeper, winking in a sly way at the Fox and the Cat, as if to say: *I see the sneaky trick you are planning.*

As soon as Pinocchio was in bed, he fell fast asleep and began to dream of gold coins growing like grapes on a vine. Just as he reached out to take some, he was awakened by the innkeeper, who told him it was midnight.

"Are my friends ready?" the Puppet asked.

"They left two hours ago."

"Why in such a hurry?"

"Unfortunately, the Cat received a message that his child was sick. There was no time to say good-bye to you."

"Did they pay for the supper?"

"How could they do such a thing? Being such fine people, they did not want you to lose the honor of paying the bill."

"Too bad! That kind of loss would have been just fine with me," said Pinocchio, scratching his head. "Where did my good friends say they would meet me?"

"At the Field of Wonders, at sunrise."

Pinocchio paid one gold coin for the suppers and started on his way to find the field that would make him rich. As he walked along in the dark, he met a tiny insect that shone with a pale, soft light.

"Who are you?" Pinocchio asked.

"I am the ghost of the Talking Cricket," answered a faint voice.

"What do you want?" asked the Puppet.

"I want to give you some good advice. Return home and give the four coins you have left to your poor old father. He is crying because he has not seen you for many days."

"Tomorrow my father will be a rich man, for I will have two thousand gold coins."

"Don't listen to those who promise you riches overnight, my boy. Most often, they are either fools or cheats! Listen to me and go home."

"But I want to go on!"

"The night is dark! And the road is very dangerous!"

"I want to go on."

"Remember this—boys who must have their own way run into trouble sooner or later."

"That is nonsense. Good-bye, Cricket Ghost."

"Good night, Pinocchio, and may Heaven keep you from the Bandits."

The little light was suddenly gone, just as if someone had blown it out. The road was dark and lonely again.

"Dear, oh, dear!" said the Puppet to himself, as he walked along. "We boys are really very unlucky. Everybody scolds us and gives us advice—*everyone*—even the Talking Cricket. *Bandits!* Phooey! I have never believed in them, and never…"

Just then, Pinocchio heard a noise behind him. There in the darkness stood two dark shadows, wrapped from head to foot in black sacks. The two figures leaped toward him as softly as ghosts.

"Maybe I was wrong about Bandits!" Pinocchio said to himself. He did not know where to hide the gold coins, so he stuck them under his tongue. He turned to run away, but something grabbed his arms.

"Out with the money or you're a dead man! After you're dead, we'll kill your father," warned a deep voice.

"Kill your father," repeated the shorter of the two Bandits.

"No, no, no, not my father!" cried Pinocchio, wild with terror. But as he screamed, the gold coins clinked together in his mouth.

"Ah! So that's the game! You have the money hidden under your tongue. Out with it!"

When Pinocchio became stubborn and would not open his mouth, the smaller Bandit pulled out a knife and tried to pry his mouth open.

Quick as a flash, the Puppet sank his teeth deep into the Bandit's hand, bit it off, and spat it out. Imagine his surprise when he saw that it was not a hand, but a *cat's paw*!

Out of shock and fear, Pinocchio tore loose from his attackers and climbed up a giant pine tree. The Bandits tried to follow him, but they slipped and fell.

Not yet ready to give up, the Bandits started a bonfire at the foot of the tree. Pinocchio saw the flames climbing higher and higher. He did not wish to become a roasted Puppet, so he jumped to the ground and began running. The Bandits were not far behind!

CHAPTER SEVEN

Lessons on Lies and Love

The chase went on all night. Just as the sun came up, Pinocchio spied a little white cottage way beyond the trees. He ran through the woods, then toward the cottage. Tired and out of breath, Pinocchio knocked on the door. No one answered. He knocked harder as he heard the Bandits' steps getting closer—still no answer.

He began to kick and bang. At last, a window opened and a lovely young girl looked out. She had blue hair and a pure, white face. Her eyes were closed and her hands crossed on her chest. In a weak voice, she whispered, "No one lives in this house. Everyone is dead. Even I am dead."

"Dead? How can you be at the window, then?"

"I am waiting for the coffin to take me away."

With these words, the girl disappeared.

"Oh, Lovely Girl with Blue Hair," cried Pinocchio, "open, I beg of you. Help a poor boy who is being chased by two Ban—"

—But strong hands grabbed him by the neck!

"Now we have you!" growled two horrible voices. "This time you shall open your mouth!"

"Well," said one of them, "let's hang him up!"

"Hang him up," repeated the other.

They dragged Pinocchio back to the edge of the woods. They held his hands behind his back

and slipped a noose around his neck. Throwing the rope over the limb of a giant oak tree, they pulled till he hung far above the ground.

Then they sat on the grass and waited. But after three hours the Puppet's eyes were still open, his mouth still shut, and his legs kicked harder than ever.

"Good-bye for now," called the Bandits. "In the morning, we hope to find you with your mouth wide open." With these words they left.

"Oh, Father, dear Father! If you were only here!" Pinocchio thought. He closed his eyes and hung there, very sad and lonely.

Luckily for Pinocchio, just at that moment, the Lovely Girl with Blue Hair looked out of her window. She saw him dangling from the faraway tree. She clapped her hands three times. A large Falcon then landed on the window ledge.

"What do you command, my good Fairy?" asked the Falcon. (For the Lovely Girl with Blue Hair was actually a very kind Fairy.)

"Fly to that Puppet hanging from the giant oak tree. With your strong beak, untie him, take him down, and lay him softly at the foot of the oak."

The Falcon flew away and after two minutes returned, saying, "I have done as you have asked."

"Was he alive or dead?"

"Still alive."

The Fairy clapped her hands twice. A magnificent Poodle appeared, walking on his back legs, dressed in a fancy uniform.

"Come, Medoro," said the Fairy. "Get my best coach ready and go to the forest. On reaching the oak tree, you will find an injured Puppet. Gently place him in the coach and bring him to me."

In a few minutes, a lovely little glass coach, with lining as soft as whipped cream, left the stable. It was drawn by one hundred pairs of white mice.

When the coach returned, the Fairy lifted the poor little Puppet in her arms, carried him to bed, and sent for the three most famous doctors.

One after another the doctors came: a Crow, an Owl, and a Talking Cricket.

"I would like to know, dear doctors," said the Fairy, "if this poor Puppet is dead or alive."

The Crow stepped out and felt Pinocchio's pulse, his nose, and his little toe.

"I think this Puppet is dead," he said, "but if by any chance he is *not*, then that would be a sure sign that he is alive!"

"I am sorry," said the Owl, "to disagree. I think this Puppet is alive. But if by any chance he is *not*, then that would be a sure sign that he is dead!"

"And what do you think?" the Fairy asked the Talking Cricket.

"I say that a wise doctor, when he does not know what he is talking about, should know enough to say nothing. However, that Puppet is not a stranger to me. I have known him a long time. He is a rascal of the worst kind!"

Pinocchio shivered, opened his eyes and closed them again.

"He is a rude, lazy runaway."

Pinocchio hid under the sheets. He slipped the coins from his mouth to his pocket. He was afraid he might swallow them if he started to sob.

"That Puppet is a naughty son who is breaking his father's heart!"

Long, shuddering sobs were heard. When the sheets were raised, they discovered Pinocchio crying huge tears!

As soon as the three doctors had left, the Fairy went to Pinocchio's bed and gave him some medicine with a glass of water.

"Now," said the Fairy lovingly, "tell me why the Bandits were after you."

Pinocchio told her all that had happened. When he got to the part about hiding the gold coins under his tongue, the Fairy became curious.

"Where are the coins now?" she asked.

"I lost them," answered Pinocchio. But *he had told a lie*, for, as we know, he had them in his pocket. As he spoke, his nose became at least two inches longer.

"And where did you lose them?"

"In the woods." And at this second lie, his nose grew a few *more* inches.

"If you lost them in the woods," said the Fairy, "we'll go and find them."

"Ah, now I remember!" replied the Puppet, becoming more and more mixed up with his own lies. "I did not lose the gold coins. I swallowed them when I drank the medicine."

At this third lie, his nose became longer than ever—so long that he almost put the Fairy's eyes out with it. This made the Fairy laugh.

"Why do you laugh?" the Puppet asked, worried now at the sight of his growing nose.

"I am laughing at your lies."

"How do you know I am lying?"

"Lies, my boy, are easy to figure out. There are two kinds of lies—lies with short legs and lies with long noses. Yours, just now, have long noses."

Pinocchio was so embarrassed that he tried to run from the room, but his nose was so long that he could not get it through the door.

The Puppet cried for hours over his nose. The Fairy was trying to teach him to stop telling lies (the worst habit *any* boy may have). But when she saw how sad he was, she felt sorry for him and clapped her hands. In through the window flew a thousand woodpeckers that landed on Pinocchio's nose. They pecked and pecked so hard at that huge nose that it was soon the same size as before.

"How good you are, my Fairy," said Pinocchio, drying his eyes, "and how much I love you!"

"I love you, too," answered the Fairy, "and if you wish to stay with me, you may be my little brother and I'll be your good sister."

"I would like to stay with you—but what about my poor father?"

"I have sent for him, and before night he will be here."

"Really?" cried Pinocchio joyfully. "Then, my good Fairy, may I go to meet him? I cannot wait to kiss that dear old man who has suffered so much because of me."

"Yes. Go ahead, but be careful you don't get lost. Take the path through the woods and you'll surely meet him."

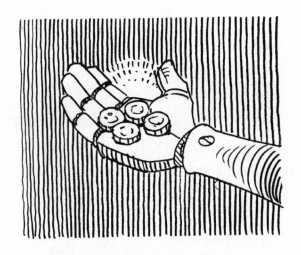

CHAPTER EIGHT

The Field of Wonders

Pinocchio left and ran to the edge of the woods like a deer. When he reached the giant oak tree he stopped, for he thought he heard a noise in the bushes. He was right. There stood the Fox and the Cat, the two "friends" who had skipped out without paying for supper at the *Red Lobster Inn*.

"Hello, dear Pinocchio!" cried the Fox, hugging him. "How did you happen to come here?"

"How did you happen to come here?" repeated the Cat.

"It is a long story," said the Puppet. "The other night, when you left me alone at the inn, I met the Bandits on the road—"

"The Bandits? Oh, my poor friend! And what did they want?"

"They wanted my gold coins."

"Rascals!" said the Fox.

"The worst sort of rascals!" added the Cat.

"I began to run," continued the Puppet, "but they caught me and hanged me from the limb of that giant oak over there."

"How terrible," said the Fox. "What an awful world to live in! Where shall we find a safe place for fine men like ourselves?"

As the Fox was talking, Pinocchio noticed that the Cat carried his right front paw in a sling.

"What happened to your paw?" he asked.

The Cat tried to answer, but he became so mixed up that the Fox had to help him out.

"My friend does not want to brag. But, about an hour ago, we met an old wolf. He was starving and begged for food. Having nothing to give him, what do you think my kind friend did? He bit off his own paw and gave it to that poor wolf."

As he spoke, the Fox wiped away a tear. Pinocchio, almost in tears himself, whispered in the Cat's ear, "If all the cats were like you, how lucky the mice would be!"

"And what are you doing here?" asked the Fox.

"I am waiting for my father."

"Where are your gold coins?"

"I still have them in my pocket, except one which I spent at the *Red Lobster Inn*."

"Just think! Those four coins could become two thousand tomorrow," said the Fox. "Why don't you plant them in the Field of Wonders?"

"No. I must meet Father…"

"Too bad. For a rich man has bought the field, and today is the last day it will be open to the public," sighed the Fox.

"Well… how far is this Field of Wonders?"

"Only two miles. You can bury the money, and, after a few minutes, gather your two thousand coins and return home rich. Are you coming?"

Pinocchio waited a moment. He remembered the good Fairy, old Geppetto, and the advice of the Talking Cricket. But finally he did what all boys do who have no heart and few brains. He gave in and agreed to go with the Fox and the Cat.

They walked for at least half a day toward the City of Foolafool. Just outside the city, they stepped into a lonely field, which looked the same as any other field.

"Here we are," said the Fox. "Dig a hole here and put the gold coins into it. Very good! Now, get some water from that stream over there and sprinkle it over the spot."

Pinocchio pulled off his shoe, filled it with water, and sprinkled it over the coins.

"Now we can go," said the Fox. "Return here within twenty minutes. You will find a vine filled with gold coins."

Pinocchio, wild with joy, walked the Cat and Fox back to town. He thanked them many times and promised them each a beautiful gift.

"We don't want any gifts," they answered. "It is enough for us that we have helped you to become rich. This makes us happy as kings."

They said good-bye to Pinocchio, wished him good luck, and went on their way.

Pinocchio could hardly wait for twenty minutes to go by. When it was finally time, he hurried toward the Field of Wonders. His heart beat faster and faster, and he kept thinking:

"What if, instead of two thousand, I should find one hundred thousand? I'll build myself a beautiful palace, with a thousand stables filled with a thousand wooden horses to play with, a cellar full of lemonade and soda, and a library of candies, fruits, cakes, and cookies."

When he came to the place where he had buried the coins, he saw—guess what! *Nothing!*

Pinocchio scratched his head to think.

Just then, he heard a burst of laughter close to his head. He turned and there, above him on the branch of a tree, sat a large Parrot, busily cleaning his feathers.

"Well," cried the Puppet angrily, "may I know, Mr. Parrot, what is so funny?"

"I am laughing at those fools who believe everything they hear, and who are caught so easily in the traps set for them."

"Do you, perhaps, mean me?"

"I certainly do mean you, poor Pinocchio—you who are such a little silly as to believe that gold can be planted in a field just like beans or peas. Don't you know that in order to have money, you must work to earn it?"

"I don't know what you are talking about," said the Puppet, beginning to tremble with fear.

"Too bad! I'll explain myself better," said the Parrot. "While you were away in the City of Foolafool, the Fox and the Cat returned here in a great hurry. They dug up your four gold coins and ran away as fast as the wind."

Pinocchio's mouth opened wide. He would not believe this and began to dig wildly at the earth, but no money was there. *Every coin was gone.*

Full of fear and worry, he ran to the city and went straight to the courthouse to report the robbery to the Judge. The Judge was a large Gorilla, old and respected. A long, white beard covered his chest.

Pinocchio told his sad tale of being robbed, and begged for justice. The Judge listened to him with great patience. When the Puppet had no more to say, the Judge put out his hand and rang a bell. At the sound, two large Bulldog guards appeared.

"This poor fool has been fooled and robbed of four gold pieces," said the Judge to the Bulldogs. "Take him, therefore, and throw him into prison."

Pinocchio, on hearing this sentence, was completely confused. He tried to argue, but the two Bulldogs clapped their paws on his mouth and hustled him away to jail.

There he stayed for four long months. And if it had not been for a very lucky chance, he probably would have been there longer. For, my dear children, it just so happened that the young emperor who ruled over the City of Foolafool had gained a great victory over his enemy. In celebration, he had ordered that all thieves should go free.

"If the others go, I go too," said Pinocchio to the jailer.

"Not you," answered the jailer. "You are a fool, not a—"

"I beg your pardon," interrupted Pinocchio, "I, too, am a thief—for I robbed *myself* of my coins."

"In that case you also are free," said the jailer, scratching his head. Pinocchio ran out and away, and never looked back.

Pinocchio raced toward the house of the lovely Fairy. Would he ever see his father and his little blue-haired sister again?

"How unhappy I have been," he said to himself. "And yet I deserve everything, for I am very stubborn! I must always have my own way. I won't listen to those who love me. But from now on, I'll be different and try to obey. I wonder if Father is waiting for me. Will I find him at the Fairy's house? And will the Fairy, who has been so good to me, ever forgive me for all I have done?"

CHAPTER NINE

The Island of the Busy Bees

Pinocchio ran and walked and ran until he reached the main road that led to the Fairy's house. He could see down into the valley far below him. There he saw the woods where he had met the Fox and the Cat, and the tall oak tree where he had been hanged. But though he searched far and near, he could not see the house where the Fairy with Blue Hair lived.

He became terribly frightened. Running as fast as he could, he finally came to the spot where the little house had once stood. But it was no longer there. In its place was a marble tombstone with the following sad words carved into it:

HERE LIES
THE LOVELY FAIRY
WITH BLUE HAIR
WHO DIED OF GRIEF
WHEN ABANDONED
BY -
HER - LITTLE BROTHER
PINOCCHIO

The poor Puppet was heartbroken. He cried all night, and was still sobbing to himself the following morning.

"Oh, my dear, dear Fairy, are you really dead? And my father—where can he be? Please, dear Fairy, tell me where he is and I shall never, never leave him again! I'm so lonely. What shall I do alone in the world? Oh, oh, oh!"

Poor Pinocchio! He tried tearing out his hair, till he remembered it was painted on. Just then, a large Pigeon flew over and saw the Puppet below.

"Tell me," cried the Pigeon, "do you by chance know of a Puppet named Pinocchio?"

"Pinocchio?" replied the Puppet, jumping to his feet. "Why, *I* am Pinocchio!"

At this answer, the Pigeon, who was very large indeed, flew swiftly down to the earth.

"Then you know Geppetto, also?" it asked.

"Do I know him? He's my poor, dear father! Has he, perhaps, told you about me? Is he still alive?"

"I left him three days ago on the shore of a large sea."

"What was he doing?"

"He was building a little boat to cross the ocean. For the last four months he has been all over Europe looking for you. He has now made up his mind to look in America, far across the ocean."

"How far is it from here to the shore where you saw him?" asked Pinocchio.

"More than fifty miles."

"Fifty miles? Oh, how I wish I had your wings!"

"If you want to go, I'll carry you."

Without another word, Pinocchio jumped onto the Pigeon's back. They flew all day and all night.

The next morning they were at the seashore. Pinocchio jumped off the Pigeon's back. And, wanting no thanks, it swiftly flew away.

The shore was full of people, screaming and tearing their hair as they looked toward the sea.

"What has happened?" Pinocchio asked a little old woman.

"A poor old father lost his only son, and today he left in a tiny boat to search for him across the ocean. The water is very rough, and we are afraid he will be drowned!"

"Where is the little boat?"

"Straight down there," answered the woman, pointing to a tiny shadow floating on the sea.

Pinocchio looked closely and cried, "It's my father! It's my father!"

The little boat appeared and disappeared in the angry waves. Pinocchio stood on a high rock and waved with hand and cap—even with his nose.

It looked as if Geppetto knew it was his son, for he took off his cap and waved back. Suddenly, caught up in a huge wave, the boat disappeared and was gone. With a frantic cry, Pinocchio dived into the sea.

"I'll save him! I'll save my father!" he shouted.

The Puppet swam like a fish in the rough water. Soon he was far away from land and completely out of sight.

"Poor boy!" cried the fishermen on the shore, mumbling a few prayers as they returned home.

Pinocchio swam all night long through a terrible storm. At dawn, he saw the sandy shore of an island in the middle of the sea, but did not have the strength left to reach it. Luckily for him, a huge wave tossed him right up onto the beach.

Little by little the sky cleared. The sun came out, and the sea became as calm as a lake. The Puppet looked for some sign of a boat with a little man in it. He saw nothing but a big fish swimming nearby, with his head far out of the water.

"Hey, there, Mr. Fish, may I have a word with you?" Pinocchio called out.

"Even two, if you want," answered the fish, who happened to be a very polite Dolphin.

"In your travels last night… did you see a little boat… with my father in it?"

"In last night's storm," answered the Dolphin, "I would think any little boat must have sunk."

"And my father?"

"By this time, he has probably been swallowed by the Terrible Whale, which has been bringing terror to these waters lately."

"Is this Whale very big?" asked Pinocchio, starting to tremble with fright.

"Is he big?" replied the Dolphin. "He is larger than a five-story building, with a mouth so big that a whole train could easily get into it."

"Oh, my!" cried the Puppet. "I must go. Farewell, Mr. Fish. Many thanks!"

Pinocchio walked around the island until he came to a small country called the Land of the Busy Bees. The streets were filled with people hurrying about, all working at something.

"I see," said Pinocchio, "this is no place for me! I was not born for work."

But he was hungry. He would either have to work or beg to get a bite to eat.

Just then a man passed by, pulling two heavy carts filled with coal.

Pinocchio begged, "Will you be so good as to give me a penny? For I am weak with hunger."

"I'll give you *four* pennies," answered the Coal Man, "if you will help me pull these two carts."

"I am shocked!" answered the Puppet. "You hurt my pride! I wish you to know I have never been a donkey, and I have never pulled a cart."

"Then, my boy," said the Coal Man, "if you are so hungry, eat two pieces of your pride."

In the next half-hour, Pinocchio begged of everyone he saw, but they all told him to look for work instead of begging in the street. Finally, a little woman went by carrying two water jugs.

"Good woman, may I have a drink from one of your jugs?" asked Pinocchio, burning with thirst.

"With pleasure, my boy!" she answered.

When Pinocchio had had enough, he grumbled that he was still hungry.

"If you help me carry one of these jugs to my home," offered the little woman, "I'll give you a slice of bread."

Pinocchio looked at the jug and said nothing.

"And with the bread, I'll give you a nice dish of cauliflower with white sauce on it. And after that, some cake and jam."

This last idea was just too good to refuse.

"Very well, I'll carry a jug home for you."

When they arrived home, the little woman fed Pinocchio all the good things she had promised. He ate everything in sight.

His hunger finally gone, he raised his head to thank the kind lady. As he looked at her, his mouth fell open and he gave a shout of surprise.

"Why all this surprise?" asked the good woman, laughing.

"B-b-because—" said Pinocchio, "because— you look like—you remind me of—yes, yes, the same voice, the same eyes, the same blue hair. Oh, *my little Fairy!* Tell me that it is you!"

Pinocchio threw himself on the floor and, crying, hugged the knees of the mysterious little woman.

CHAPTER TEN

Pinocchio Goes to School

The woman thought Pinocchio would melt away if he cried much longer, so she finally told him that she *was* the little Fairy with Blue Hair.

"You naughty Puppet! How did you know me?" she asked, laughing.

"My love for you told me who you were."

"Do you remember? You left me when I was a little girl and now you find me a grown woman. I am so old, I could almost be your mother!"

"I am very glad of that, for then I can call you 'mother' instead of 'sister.' For a long time I have wanted a mother, just like other boys. But how did you grow up so quickly?"

"That's a secret!"

"Tell it to me. I also want to grow a little. Look at me! I have never grown an inch."

"But you can't grow," answered the Fairy. "Puppets never grow."

"Oh, I'm tired of always being a Puppet!" cried Pinocchio disgustedly. "It's about time for me to grow into a man as everyone else does."

"And you will if you deserve it—"

"Really? What can I do to deserve it?"

"It's very simple. Try to be a good boy."

"Don't you think I try?"

"Far from it! Good boys love to study and work, but you—"

"I am lazy all year round."

"Good boys always obey and tell the truth."

"And I always disobey and tell lies."

"Good boys go gladly to school."

"And I hate school. But, dear Fairy, from now on I'll be different."

"Do you promise?"

"I promise. I want to become a good boy and help my father. Where is my poor father now?"

"I do not know."

"Will I ever find him and hug him once more?"

"I think so. Yes, I am sure of it."

"Oh, how happy that makes me," cried Pinocchio, kissing the Fairy's hands. "Tell me, little Mother, it isn't true that you are dead, is it?"

"It doesn't seem so," said the Fairy, smiling.

"If you only knew how I cried when I read *'Here lies—'* "

"I do know, and because your sadness showed that you have a kind heart, I have forgiven you. There is always hope for boys with kind hearts, even though they are sometimes naughty. This is the reason I have come so far to look for you. From now on, I'll be your own little mother."

"Oh! How lovely!" cried Pinocchio, jumping with joy.

"Will you obey me always and do as I wish?"

"Gladly! More than gladly!"

"Beginning tomorrow," said the Fairy, "will you go to school every day and after that find a job you like?"

Pinocchio looked quite unhappy and serious.

"I was just thinking," whined the Puppet, "that it seems too late for me to go to school now."

"No, indeed, dear Pinocchio. Remember it is never too late to learn."

"But I don't want any kind of a job."

"Why?"

"Because work wears me out!"

"My dear boy," said the Fairy, "no one can find happiness without work. No good comes to lazy boys!"

These words touched Pinocchio's heart, and he said seriously, "I'll work. I'll study. I'll do all you tell me. I am sick and tired of being a Puppet. No matter how hard it is, I want to become a boy. You promise me that I will?"

"Yes, I promise, but now it is up to you."

In the morning, bright and early, Pinocchio started for school.

When the boys saw a Puppet enter the classroom, they laughed until they cried. Everyone played tricks on him. One even tried to tie strings to his feet and his hands to make him dance about the room.

Finally, Pinocchio got tired of these tricksters.

"Careful, boys," he said threateningly. "I haven't come here to be made fun of. I'll respect you and I want you to respect me."

"Hurrah for Dr. Know-it-all!" howled the boys, bursting with laughter. One of them put out his hand to pull the Puppet's nose.

But he was not quick enough. Pinocchio stretched his leg under the table and kicked him hard on the ankle.

"Oh, what hard feet!" cried the boy.

From then on, the boys stopped their tricks and began to like Pinocchio. Even the teacher came to like him, and often praised him, for he saw that he was trying to be a good student.

Pinocchio's only fault was that he had too *many* friends, and some were the worst pranksters in the school.

"Take care, Pinocchio!" warned the teacher. "Those bad playmates will sooner or later make you lose your love for study. And they will lead you into trouble."

"There's no such danger," answered the Puppet, pointing to his forehead as if to say: *I'm too wise*. But it happened that one day he found he was not as wise as he thought.

"Have you heard the news?" shouted Pinocchio's friends one morning. "A Whale as big as a mountain has been seen near the shore."

"Really? I wonder if it could be the same one I heard of when my father was drowned!"

"We are going to see it. Are you coming?"

"No, not I. I must go to school."

"What do you care about school? You can go there tomorrow."

"And what will the teacher say?"

"Let him talk. He is paid to grumble all day."

"And my mother?"

"Mothers don't know anything," answered the scamps.

"Do you know what I'll do?" said Pinocchio. "I *will* see that Whale—but I'll go after school. I can see him then as well as now."

"Poor fool!" cried one of the boys. "Do you think that a fish like that will wait around all day for you?"

"How long does it take to get from here to the shore?" asked the Puppet.

"One hour there and back."

"Very well, then. Let's see who gets there first!" cried Pinocchio.

Across the fields they raced, with their books under their arms. Pinocchio led the way.

Poor boy! If he had only known then the awful things that were to happen to him, all because he did not listen to his teacher and his good mother.

CHAPTER ELEVEN

Troubles and More Troubles

Going like the wind, Pinocchio soon came to the shore, but there was no sign of a Whale.

"Hey, there, boys! Where's that Whale?" he asked his playmates.

"He has gone for his breakfast," laughed one.

"Or perhaps he went to bed for a little nap," said another, laughing also.

"What's the joke?" Pinocchio demanded.

The boys laughed even more. They said they were tired of him being the teacher's pet, making the rest of them look bad. They wanted him to hate books and teachers, so they had fooled him into skipping school and going with them.

This made Pinocchio angry. He called the boys names and began thumbing his nose at them. Now *they* were mad, too, and started to throw their books at him. But Pinocchio moved too quickly. The books missed him, landed in the sea, and disappeared.

At the noise, a large Crab crawled slowly out of the water. With a voice that sounded like a trombone suffering from a cold, he cried, "Stop fighting, you rascals! These battles between boys never end well. Trouble is sure to come to you!"

"Keep quiet, ugly Crab!" answered Pinocchio. "It would be better for you to chew a few cough drops to get rid of that cold you have."

In the meantime, when the boys ran out of their own books, they pulled a huge, heavy arithmetic book from Pinocchio's book bag, which was lying on the ground. One of them threw it with all his strength at Pinocchio's head. But instead of hitting the Puppet, the book struck one of the other boys, who, as white as a ghost, cried out faintly, "Oh, Mama, help! I'm dying!" and fell to the ground.

Seeing what they had done, the boys were so frightened that they ran away and disappeared.

All except Pinocchio. Forgetting his fear, he ran to the sea, soaked his handkerchief in the cool water, and with it bathed the head of his poor little schoolmate.

"Eugene! My poor Eugene!" he sobbed. "Open your eyes and look at me! Believe me, I was not the one who hit you. Oh, if only I had gone to school! Why did I listen to those boys? The teacher told me—and my mother, too!—'Beware of bad playmates!' But I'm stubborn and always I do as I wish. Oh, dear! What will become of me?"

Suddenly he heard heavy footsteps. He looked up and saw two tall officers standing over him. Pinocchio told them that he was helping his schoolmate who had been struck in the head with *his* book, but that he was not to blame.

Well, as you can imagine, the officers did not believe *that* story. They grabbed at Pinocchio to arrest him. But the Puppet stuck his little cap between his teeth and, like a bullet out of a gun, raced away toward the sea.

Seeing that it would be very hard to catch him, the officers sent a large Guard Dog after him. Pinocchio ran fast.

The Dog ran faster!

Pinocchio heard the heavy panting of Alidoro (that was the Guard Dog's name) close behind him. Luckily, he was very near the shore.

As soon as he got to the beach, Pinocchio leaped into the water. Alidoro was running too fast to stop, and he, too, landed far out in the sea. The Dog could not swim. He barked wildly:

"I am drowning! Help, Pinocchio! Save me from death!"

At those cries of suffering, the kindhearted Puppet felt sorry for poor Alidoro. He turned toward him, saying, "If I help you, will you promise to stop chasing me?"

"I promise! I promise!"

Pinocchio remembered his father had said that a kind deed is never forgotten. So he swam to Alidoro and dragged him by the tail to the shore.

"Good-bye, little Pinocchio, and thank you!" called the Dog. "You did me a favor, and if ever you need me, I shall do one for you."

Pinocchio went on swimming. Looking up and down the shore, he saw some smoke coming from the opening of a cave. Hoping he could dry his clothes and warm himself by a fire that must be in the cave, Pinocchio swam to the rocks.

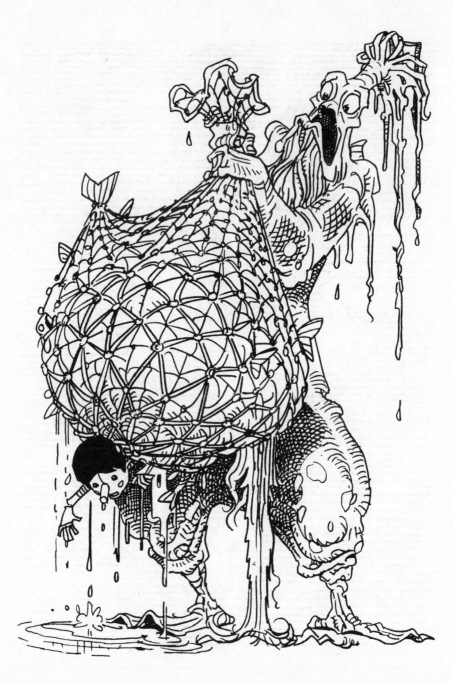

Suddenly he felt something lifting him up higher and higher. He tried to escape, but he was too late. He was caught in a huge net, among fish of all shapes and sizes.

Pinocchio spied a Fisherman just outside the cave—a Fisherman so ugly that he looked more like a sea monster. In place of hair, a thick bush of green grass covered his head. His skin was green. His eyes were green. Even his long beard that hung down to his feet was green! He looked like a giant lizard with legs and arms.

When the Fisherman pulled the net out of the sea, he cried out joyfully, "Thank Heaven! Once more I'll have a fine meal of fish!"

"Thank Heaven! I'm not a fish!" thought Pinocchio.

The Fisherman took the net of fish into the cave, where a pan of oil sizzled over a smoky fire.

"Now, let's see what kind of fish we have caught today," said the Green Fisherman. He put a hand as big as a shovel into the net and began tossing fish of all kinds—mullet, bass, whitefish, and crabs—into a large tub. But when he pulled the *last* one out, his green eyes opened wide with surprise—for it was Pinocchio!

"What kind of fish is this? I don't remember ever eating anything like it. It looks like some kind of crab."

This upset Pinocchio. "What nonsense! I am not a crab! I am a Puppet."

"A Puppet?" asked the Fisherman. "I've never eaten a Puppet fish."

"Can't you see I'm *not* a fish?" cried Pinocchio. "Now, set me free so I may return home!"

"Are you fooling? Do you think that I want to miss the chance to taste a Puppet fish? I'll fry you in the pan with the others."

Tears poured from Pinocchio's eyes.

"I should have stayed in school!" he cried. "I listened to my playmates and now I am in trouble again! Oh! Oh! Oh!"

Paying no attention to his cries, the Green Fisherman threw the Puppet into the tub.

Then he rolled the fish and Pinocchio in flour until they were completely white. One by one, the Fisherman began dropping the fish into the pot of hot oil. Pinocchio, seeing that he was next, screamed and begged for mercy.

But the ugly Green Fisherman took him by the head and—

CHAPTER TWELVE

Learning... Slowly... Slowly...

—Pinocchio closed his eyes and waited for a terrible death.

Suddenly a large Dog ran into the cave.

"Get out!" cried the Fisherman, still holding the flour-covered Puppet.

But the poor, hungry Dog wagged his tail and whined, "Give me a bite of the fish and I'll leave."

"Get out, I say!" growled the Fisherman.

At that moment, Alidoro heard a little voice cry, "Save me, Alidoro. If you don't, I fry!"

The Dog knew it was Pinocchio's voice, but was surprised that it had come from the white bundle of flour that the Fisherman held in his hand.

Then what did Alidoro do? With one great leap, he took that bundle lightly in his mouth and flew out the door! When he came to the road that led to the village, Alidoro dropped Pinocchio softly to the ground.

"How much I do thank you!" said the Puppet.

"Glad to help," answered the Dog. "You saved me once, and what is given is always returned. We are in this world to help one another."

Alidoro held out his paw to the Puppet, and the two friends said good-bye.

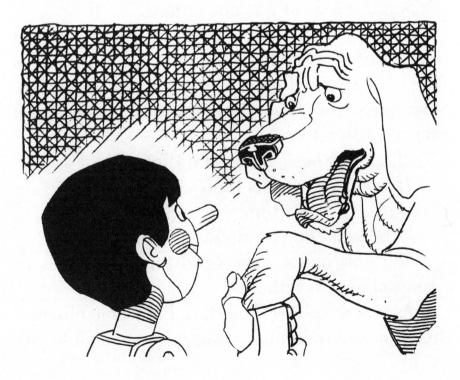

Pinocchio, left alone, walked toward a little cabin next to the road, where an old man sat at the door sunning himself.

"Tell me, good man," Pinocchio asked, "have you heard anything of a poor boy, named Eugene, with a wounded head?"

"Why, yes! The boy was brought to this cabin and now—"

"Now he is dead?" Pinocchio broke in sadly.

"No, he is alive and has returned home."

"Really? Really?" cried the Puppet with joy. "Then the wound was not serious?"

"But it might have been," answered the old man, "for a heavy book was thrown at the boy's head by a schoolmate of his, named Pinocchio. I've heard this Pinocchio is a mischief-maker, a beggar, a street rascal—"

"Lies! All lies!" screamed Pinocchio.

"Do you know this Pinocchio?"

"Um… I know him when I see him."

"And what do you think of him?"

"I think he's a very good boy who loves to study, obeys his father—"

As he was telling these lies, Pinocchio touched his nose and found it *twice as long* as it should be!

"Don't listen to me, good man!" cried Pinocchio, scared out of his wits. "These things I've said are not true at all. I know Pinocchio well and he is indeed a very bad, lazy fellow! Instead of going to school, he runs away with his playmates to have a good time."

As quickly as he spoke these words, his nose returned to its normal size.

"Why are you so pale and white?" the old man asked suddenly.

"Let me tell you. Without knowing it, I rubbed myself against a newly painted white wall," he lied, ashamed to say that he had been rolled in flour to be fried. And his nose grew again!

"What have you done with your coat and your hat and your pants?"

"I met thieves and they robbed me," Pinocchio lied again. He was ashamed to admit that the seawater had turned his tattered paper clothes and dough cap to mush. And he did not care if his nose grew still more. "Tell me, my good man. Do you, perhaps, have a little suit to give me, so that I may go home?"

"My boy, I have only this empty grain bag. If you want it, take it."

Pinocchio grabbed the bag and cut a big hole at the top and two at the sides. He pulled it on like a shirt and started out toward the village.

Along the way he began to worry.

"Will my good Fairy ever forgive this last trick of mine? I am sure she won't. And I deserve it, as usual! For I am a bad boy, always making promises that I never keep!"

He came to the village late at night. It was dark and pouring rain. He went straight to the Fairy's house and knocked at the door.

He waited and waited. Finally, after a half-hour, the fourth-floor window opened and a large Snail looked out. A tiny light glowed on top of her head. "Who knocks at this late hour?" she called.

"Is the Fairy home?" asked the Puppet.

"The Fairy is asleep and does not wish to be bothered. Who are you?"

"Pinocchio."

"Who is Pinocchio?"

"The Puppet—who lives at the Fairy's house."

"Oh, I see," said the Snail. "Wait for me there. I'll come down to open the door for you."

"Hurry, I beg of you, for I am dying of cold."

"My boy, I am a snail. Snails do not hurry."

Two hours went by. Pinocchio, trembling with fear and shivering from the cold rain, knocked a second time, louder than before.

At that second knock, a window on the third floor opened and the same Snail looked out.

"Dear little Snail," cried Pinocchio from the street. "I have been waiting two hours for you! Hurry, please!"

"My dear boy," answered the Snail in a calm, peaceful voice, "I am a snail and snails are never in a hurry." And the window closed.

Two more hours went by, and the door still remained closed!

Then Pinocchio, losing all patience, kicked the door so hard that his foot went straight through it. No matter how he tried, he could not pull it out. There he stayed the rest of the night.

As the sun was coming up, the door finally opened. That little Snail had taken exactly *nine hours* to go from the fourth floor to the street. How she must have raced!

"What are you doing with your foot through the door?" she asked the Puppet, laughing.

"It was an accident. Won't you please, pretty little Snail, ask the Fairy to help me!"

"The Fairy is asleep…"

Pinocchio, now weak and in pain, fainted and fell to the ground. When he woke up, he found himself stretched out on a sofa, and the Fairy was seated near him.

"Once more, I forgive you," said the Fairy. "But be careful not to get into mischief again."

Pinocchio promised to study and to behave himself. And he kept his word. At the end of that school year, his report card was so good that the Fairy said to him happily:

"Tomorrow your wish will come true."

"And what wish is that?"

"Tomorrow you will no longer be a Puppet. You will become a *real boy*."

Pinocchio was filled with joy. He wanted to have a party and invite his schoolmates! The Fairy promised to prepare two hundred cups of milk and four hundred slices of toast buttered on both sides.

It should have been a happy time, however—

(Sadly, in a Puppet's life there's always a "*however*" which often spoils everything.)

CHAPTER THIRTEEN

The Wonderful Land of Fun

When he had gotten over his excitement, Pinocchio wanted to pass out invitations.

"Indeed," said the Fairy, "you may invite your friends to tomorrow's party. But remember to return home before dark. Do you understand?"

"Yes, I promise," answered the Puppet.

"Take care, Pinocchio! Boys give promises very easily, but they forget them just as easily."

"But I am not like those others. When I give my word, I keep it."

Without another word, the Puppet left the house, singing and dancing. After an hour, all his friends, except one, had accepted his invitation.

There was one friend whom Pinocchio had not found at home. Everyone called him Lampwick, for he was long and thin, like the wick of an oil lamp. Lampwick was the laziest mischief-maker in the school, but he was Pinocchio's best friend.

Pinocchio searched everywhere, and finally found Lampwick hiding in a farmer's field.

"What are you doing there?" asked Pinocchio.

"I am waiting to go—"

"Where?"

"Far, far away! What do you want from me?"

"Haven't you heard my good news? Tomorrow I will no longer be a Puppet. I will become a real boy, like you."

"Good luck to you!"

"Will you come to my party tomorrow?"

"I'm telling you—at midnight I'm leaving!"

"And where are you going?"

"To the most wonderful place in the world! It's called the Land of Fun. Why don't you come, too?"

"I? Oh, no!"

"You'll be sorry if you don't come, Pinocchio. In the Land of Fun there are no schools, no teachers, and no books! Boys do nothing but play every day. That is the place for me!"

"Hmm—!" Pinocchio nodded his wooden head, as if to say: *Just the kind of life that I would like!*

"Do you want to go with me, then? Yes or no? You must make up your mind."

"No, no, no! I have promised my kind Fairy to be a good boy, and I want to keep my word. I must leave you and run. If I'm not home by dark, the Fairy will scold me."

"Let her scold. After she gets tired, she will stop," said Lampwick.

"Are you going alone or with others?"

"There will be more than a hundred boys. At midnight the wagon passes here that will take us to that happy, fun land. Stay here a while longer and you will see us!"

Poor Pinocchio. The more Lampwick tempted him, the weaker he became. He wanted to keep his promise to the Fairy... Oh, but the thought of no school, no teachers, and no books! Vacation the whole year! Oh, dear, what to do? The longer he waited to decide, the lower the sun sank in the sky. Then, using all his willpower, he said, "No, no. I want to return home, but... since it's getting dark and I'm already late, I'll wait until midnight to say good-bye to you."

The night became darker and darker. All at once, in the distance a small light twinkled.

"There it is!" cried Lampwick, jumping up.

"What?" whispered Pinocchio.

"The wagon coming to get me. For the last time, are you coming or not?"

"But is it really true that in this Land of Fun boys *never* have to study?"

"Never, never, never!"

"What a wonderful, beautiful, place! Oh—h—h!"

Finally the wagon arrived, drawn by twenty-four donkeys of all different colors. The strangest thing of all was that those donkeys, instead of iron horseshoes, wore laced shoes made of leather, just like the ones boys wear.

The wagon was driven by a little fat man, much wider than he was tall, with a smiling face that shone like an apple. Any boy who saw the Little Man loved him, and wanted to ride in his wagon to the Land of Fun.

In fact, the wagon was already filled with boys of all ages, piled one on top of the other. But they all seemed happy.

As soon as the wagon stopped, the Little Man turned to Lampwick. With bows and smiles, he asked in a sly, sweet tone, "Tell me, my fine boy, do you also want to come to my wonderful land?"

"Indeed I do," shouted Lampwick, leaping on top of the wagon.

"What about you, my dear?" asked the Little Man, turning to Pinocchio. "Will you come with us or stay here?"

"I will stay here," answered Pinocchio. "I want to return home. I would rather study and succeed in life."

"Good luck!"

"Pinocchio!" Lampwick called out. "Listen to me. Come with us and we'll always be happy."

"No, no, no!"

"Come with us and we'll always be happy," shouted all the boys in the wagon.

Pinocchio thought, and thought, and thought. He wanted to do the right thing, but—

Finally, he gave in and cried, "Make room for me! I want to go, too!"

"The seats are filled," answered the Little Man.

"I'll ride one of these donkeys," cried Pinocchio, and with one leap, he landed on a donkey's back.

As the wagon started on its way, the Puppet thought he heard a voice whispering to him:

"Poor silly! You have made a bad choice, and you are going to be a sorry boy before very long."

Pinocchio looked around to see where the words had come from, but he saw no one.

After a mile or so, Pinocchio heard the same faint voice. "Remember, little foolish one, boys who turn their backs on school and books just to have fun, sooner or later come to sadness. Believe me, *I* know! A day will come when you will be crying, just as I am crying now—but it will be too late!"

At these words, the Puppet grew more and more frightened. He jumped to the ground, ran up to the donkey he had been riding, and looked at him. Think how surprised he was when he saw that the donkey was crying—just like a boy!

"Hey, Mr. Driver!" cried the Puppet. "This donkey is crying. Did you teach him to speak?"

"No. He learned a few words when he lived for three years with a band of performing dogs."

"Poor animal!"

"Come on!" said the driver. "Don't fuss over a crying donkey. Get on his back and let's go." And he started the wagon again.

Toward dawn, they finally reached that much-dreamed-of place, the Land of Fun.

This great land was like no other in the world! Everywhere there were young boys. Some played ball, some hopscotch, some marbles. Others rode bicycles or wooden horses. Some played at hide and seek, and some played circus. A few turned somersaults and others walked on their hands. On the walls of the houses, written with crayons, were words like these:

HURRAY FER THE LAND OF FUN!
FOOEY ON ARITHMUTIK!
WE AIN'T GOT NO MORE SKOOL!!

Who could be happier than these boys? With all the candy and games and parties, the weeks passed like lightning.

"Oh, what a beautiful life this is!" said Pinocchio each time he met his friend Lampwick.

"Was I right or wrong?" answered Lampwick. "And to think you did not want to come! All of your happiness you owe to me. You see, only true friends count. Am I right?"

"It's true, Lampwick, it's true. If today I am a really happy boy, it is all because of you. And to think that the teacher used to warn me that you were a bad playmate. He even said that you would lead me into trouble."

"Poor teacher!" answered Lampwick. "I know how he enjoyed saying bad things about me. But I have a big heart, and I gladly forgive him."

"You are a kind soul," said Pinocchio, putting his arm around his friend.

Five months passed and the boys went on playing and enjoying themselves from morning till night, without ever reading even one book.

But, my children, there came a day when Pinocchio got a big surprise—a surprise which made him very unhappy, as you shall see.

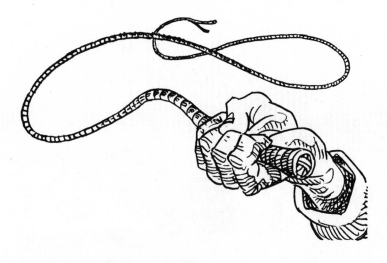

CHAPTER FOURTEEN

Leading a Donkey's Life

What was this unhappy surprise? I will tell you, dear readers. Upon awakening one morning, Pinocchio put his hand up to his head and there he found—Guess!

He found that, during the night, his ears had grown at least ten inches and turned into *donkey's ears!* He began to cry and scream. The longer he screamed, the longer grew the ears.

Hearing all the noise, a Dormouse came into the room—a wise little Dormouse, who lived upstairs. Seeing Pinocchio so upset, she felt his forehead with her little paws, then looked at him very sadly.

"My friend, I am sorry, but I must give you some very sad news. You have a very bad fever—the donkey fever."

"I don't know anything about that fever," answered the Puppet, beginning to fear what might be happening to him.

"Then I will tell you all about it," said the Dormouse. "Within two or three hours, you will no longer be a Puppet, nor a boy. You will become a real donkey."

"Oh, what have I done? What have I done?"

"My dear boy," answered the Dormouse, "the Law of Wisdom states that all lazy boys who hate school, and spend all their time playing, must sooner or later turn into donkeys. You should have thought about this before."

"But it's not my fault. Believe me, little Dormouse, the fault is all Lampwick's."

"And who is this Lampwick?"

"A classmate of mine. I wanted to return home and go to school, but Lampwick said to me, 'Why do you want to go to school? Come with me to the Land of Fun, where we'll never study and be happy from morning till night.' "

"And why did you listen to that false friend?"

"Why? Because, my dear little Dormouse, I am a foolish, heartless Puppet. Oh! If I only had a bit of heart, I would never have left that kind, loving Fairy! And by this time, I would have become a real boy! Oh, if I see Lampwick I am going to tell him what I think of him!"

After this speech, Pinocchio walked to the door of the room. But when he remembered his donkey ears, he felt ashamed to be seen, and turned back. He took a large cotton bag from a shelf, put it on his head, and went out the door.

Peeking out now and then from under the bag, he walked over and knocked at Lampwick's door.

"Who is it?" asked Lampwick from within.

"It is I!" answered the Puppet.

"Wait a minute."

After a full half-hour the door opened. There in the room stood his friend, with a large cotton bag on *his* head.

At the sight of that bag, Pinocchio thought, "I wonder if my friend, too, has donkey fever?"

But pretending he had seen nothing, he asked with a smile, "How are you, my dear Lampwick?"

"Very well. Just as happy as can be."

"Is that really true?"

"Why should I lie to you?"

"I beg your pardon, my friend, but why then are you wearing that cotton bag over your ears?"

"The doctor has ordered it because one of my knees hurts. And you, dear Puppet, why are you wearing that cotton bag down to your nose?"

"The doctor has ordered it for my hurt foot."

"Oh, my poor Pinocchio!"

"Oh, my poor Lampwick!"

Neither of the two believed the other, however. Finally they agreed to remove the bags from their heads. When they saw that each of them had grown donkey's ears, they began to make fun of each other, and burst into laughter.

All of a sudden Lampwick stopped laughing. He staggered and almost fell. Pale as a ghost, he cried, "Help, Pinocchio! I can no longer stand up!"

"I can't either," cried Pinocchio, his laughter turning to tears.

They had hardly finished speaking, when both of them fell on their hands and knees and began running and jumping around the room. As they ran, their arms turned into legs, their faces grew long snouts, and their backs became covered with long, gray hairs.

But the most horrible moment came when their tails appeared. Overcome with shame and sadness, they tried to cry and moan, but, instead, burst forth into loud donkey snorts:

"Hee-haw! Hee-haw! Hee-haw!"

At that moment, there was a loud knock at the door. "Open!" cried a voice. "I am the Little Man, the wagon driver who brought you here. Open, I say, or beware!"

The two sad and confused little fellows just stood and looked at each other. Outside the room, the Little Man grew tired of waiting and kicked open the door. With his usual sweet smile, he spoke to Pinocchio and Lampwick.

"Fine work, boys! You have hee-hawed so well that I knew your voices right away."

On hearing this, the two Donkeys bowed their heads in shame, dropped their ears, and put their tails between their legs.

After combing their hairy coats smooth, the Little Man put ropes around their necks and led them to a marketplace far away from the Land of Fun, hoping to sell them at a good price.

He did not have to wait very long for an offer. Lampwick was bought by a farmer whose donkey had died the day before. Pinocchio was sold to the owner of a circus, who wanted to teach him to do tricks for his audiences.

And now, my young readers, do you understand how the Little Man earned money? This horrible man went around the world looking for boys—lazy boys, boys who hated books and school and wanted to run away. He took them with him to the Land of Fun. When, after months of all play and no work, they became little donkeys, he sold them at the marketplace. In a few years, he had become a millionaire.

What happened to Lampwick? My dear children, I can not say. Pinocchio, I can tell you, suffered greatly.

His new master put him in a stable with only hay to eat. Pinocchio spit it out, crying, "Hee-haw! Hee-haw! Hee-haw! I can't eat this stuff!"

But poor Pinocchio was starving, so he tried the hay. "It isn't much like macaroni, but it's not bad," he said to himself. "But how much happier I would be if I had studied! Instead of hay, I could be eating some good bread and butter."

When his master returned, he said, "Now, little donkey, you are to help me earn some fine gold coins, do you hear? Come along. I am going to teach you to jump, and bow, and dance, and even to stand on your head."

After three long months, Pinocchio had learned all the tricks. His master put signs up all around the town announcing a special show.

Great Show Tonight!
Leaps and Stunts by Great Acrobats
The Famous Dancing Horses of Italy
And Introducing the Famous Donkey
PINOCCHIO

That night, the theater was packed with children who could hardly wait to see the Famous Donkey dance.

When the first part of the performance was over, the Circus Owner, in a black coat, white knee pants, and black leather boots, came out and announced that Pinocchio would be the next act.

The clapping began and grew to a roar when Pinocchio, the Famous Donkey, entered the circus ring. He wore a new bridle of shining leather with buckles of polished brass. Two white flowers were tied to his ears. Ribbons and tassels of red silk decorated his mane, which was twisted into many curls. A wide belt of gold and silver was fastened around his waist, and his tail was decorated with brightly colored ribbons. He was a handsome Donkey indeed!

The Owner bowed, then turned to Pinocchio, saying, "Pinocchio, greet your audience!"

Pinocchio bent his two front knees to the ground and remained kneeling until the Owner, with the crack of the whip, cried sharply:

"Walk!" The Donkey lifted himself and walked around the ring.

"Trot!" Pinocchio changed his step.

"Full speed!" Pinocchio ran as fast as he could.

All at once the Owner raised his arm and a pistol shot rang out. The little Donkey fell to the ground "dead." A shower of shouts and clapping greeted the Donkey as he got to his feet.

At all that noise, Pinocchio lifted his head and raised his eyes. There, in the front row, sat a beautiful woman. Around her neck she wore a long gold chain, from which hung a large locket. On the locket was painted the picture of a Puppet.

"That picture is of me! That beautiful lady is my Fairy!" said Pinocchio to himself. He felt so happy that he tried his best to cry out to her.

But instead of words, a loud, snorting hee-haw was heard in the theater. The audience burst out laughing at him. And even worse, he looked up and saw that the Fairy had disappeared!

He felt himself fainting, and his eyes filled with tears. No one paid any attention, however, and the Owner, cracking his whip, cried out:

"Bravo, Pinocchio! Now show us how you can jump through the rings."

Pinocchio tried, but, as he did so, his back legs caught in the ring and he fell to the floor. When he got up, he was lame and could hardly limp as far as the stable.

The next morning the animal doctor said that he would be lame for the rest of his life.

"What do I want with a lame donkey?" said the Owner. "I'll throw him in the ocean and drown him. Then I can at least use his leather for a drumhead."

CHAPTER FIFTEEN

Pinocchio Finds His Father

And so the owner took him to a high cliff overlooking the sea. There, he put a stone around his neck, tied a rope to one of his back feet, and pushed him off the cliff into the water.

And was that the end of Pinocchio? Oh, no, children. For Pinocchio had a mother, and, like all mothers who love their children, she never lost sight of him. This good Fairy saw him in danger of drowning and sent a thousand fishes to the spot where he lay. They thought he was really a dead donkey and began to eat him. When only his wooden bones were left, they swam away—and Pinocchio was once again a Puppet.

Pinocchio rose to the top of the sea and then swam for a long time. Finally, he saw a large, white rock in the middle of the sea. High on the rock stood a little Goat, calling for the Puppet to come to her. Her coat was a bright blue color that reminded him of the hair of the lovely girl.

Pinocchio swam toward the white rock—but suddenly, a horrible sea monster stuck its head out of the water! A huge head with a huge mouth, filled with rows of gleaming teeth!

Do you know what it was?

That sea monster was the same Terrible Whale which you have heard of before in this story.

Poor Pinocchio! He swam faster, but that giant mouth kept coming nearer and nearer.

"Hurry, Pinocchio, I beg you!" cried the little Goat, holding a hoof out to help him.

But, dear children, it was too late. The monster caught the Puppet, who soon found himself sliding past the gleaming white teeth, right down into the black darkness of the Whale's stomach!

"Help! Help!" he cried.

"Who is there to help you, unhappy boy?" said a rough voice.

"Who is talking?" asked Pinocchio fearfully.

"A poor Tuna swallowed by the Whale at the same time as you," answered the voice. "And what kind of a fish are you?"

"I am no fish. I am a Puppet."

"If you are not a fish, why did you let this monster swallow you?"

"I didn't let him. He chased me and swallowed me without talking it over with me. And now I must escape! How big is this Whale?"

"His body, not counting the tail, is almost a *mile* long!"

At that, Pinocchio thought there was no hope. But then he saw a faint light in the distance.

"What can that be?" he said. "If it's a way out of here, I'm going to find it. Good-bye, Tuna."

"Good-bye, Puppet, and good luck."

"When shall I see you again?" Pinocchio asked.

"Who knows? It is better not to think about it," answered the sad Tuna.

Pinocchio sloshed along in the darkness toward the distant light. On and on he went till finally he found—I give you a thousand guesses, my dear children! He found a little dinner table lit by a candle stuck in a glass bottle. At the table sat a little old man, eating fish.

At this sight, the poor Puppet screamed with joy and threw his arms around the surprised old man's neck.

"Oh, Father, dear Father! Have I found you at last? Now I shall never, never leave you again!"

"Is it true?" answered the old man, rubbing his eyes. "Are you really my own dear Pinocchio?"

"Yes, yes, yes! And you have forgiven me, haven't you? Oh, my dear Father, how good you are. Oh, but if you only knew how many troubles I have had!"

Pinocchio told his father everything that had happened to him, and how he had seen a poor man drowning in the sea. "I knew that little man was you," he cried, "because my heart told me so, and I waved to you from the shore."

"I knew you also," said Geppetto, "and I wanted to go to you—but how could I? The sea was too rough and my boat was sinking. Then a Terrible Whale came out of the sea and swallowed me as easily as if I had been a peppermint. That was two long years ago, my Pinocchio."

"And how have you lived, dear Father?" asked Pinocchio in wonder. "Where did you find the candle? And matches? And food?"

"The same storm which flooded my boat also sunk a large ship. The sailors were all saved, but the same Terrible Whale that swallowed me, swallowed that ship."

"What! Swallowed a *whole* ship?"

"At one gulp. Luckily for me, that ship was loaded with food, water, some candles, and boxes of matches, and I have been able to live for these two years. But now I am down to the very last crumbs, and this candle is the last one I have."

"Then, my dear Father," said Pinocchio, "there is no time to lose. We must try to escape."

"Escape! How?"

"We can run out of the Whale's mouth and dive into the sea."

"But I cannot swim, my dear Pinocchio."

"Don't worry. You can climb on my shoulders. I am a fine swimmer and will carry you safely to the shore. Let me try! And even if we die, we shall at least die together."

With that, Pinocchio picked up the candle and led the way through the stomach of the Whale. When they reached the throat of the monster, they stopped and waited for the right time to escape.

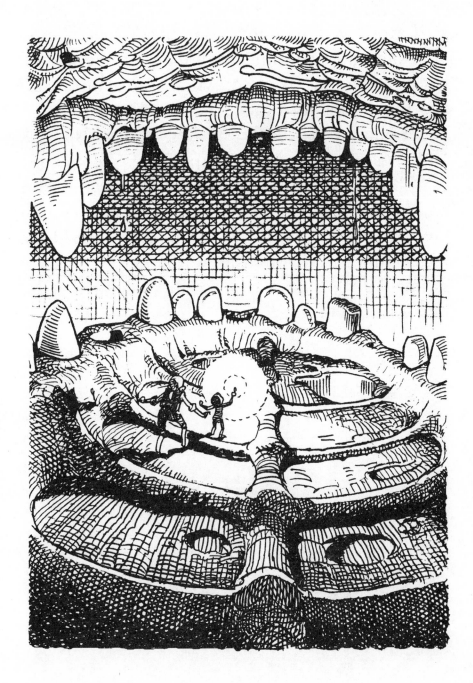

I want you to know that the Whale, being very old and suffering from allergies, slept with his mouth open. And so, when Pinocchio heard the Whale begin to snore, he saw his chance.

"Follow me closely, Father," he whispered. "The time has come to escape."

They climbed up the throat of the monster and came to that huge open mouth. When Geppetto had climbed onto his shoulders, Pinocchio dived into the water and started to swim. The Whale was so sound asleep that he never heard a thing.

CHAPTER SIXTEEN

A Real Change of Heart

On and on swam Pinocchio. He tried to stay calm and brave, but his strength was leaving him. He felt he could not go on much longer, and the shore was still far away. He turned to Geppetto and cried out weakly:

"Help me, Father! Help, for I am dying!"

Just then a voice called from the sea:

"Who is there? What is the trouble?"

"It is I and my poor father."

"I know the voice. You are Pinocchio."

"Yes! And you?"

"I am the Tuna who was with you in the Whale's stomach."

"And how did you escape?"

"I watched what you did. You showed me the way and I followed."

"Tuna, you came just in time! I beg you! Help us, or we are lost!"

"With great pleasure indeed. Climb on my back. Soon you will be safe on land."

As soon as they reached the shore, Pinocchio turned to the fish, saying, "Dear friend, you have saved my father. Let me show you how grateful I am." Pinocchio knelt on the sand and kissed him on his cheek. The Tuna turned quickly to hide his tears and disappeared into the sea.

Pinocchio turned to his old, sick father. "Lean on my arm, dear Father," he said, "and let us look for a house where we might get a bite to eat."

They had not taken a hundred steps when they saw two ragged creatures sitting on a stone, begging for money.

It was the Fox and the Cat, but one could hardly recognize them, they looked so miserable. The Cat, after making believe he was blind for so many years, really *had* lost the sight of both eyes. And the Fox, old, thin, and almost hairless, had even sold his tail for a bite to eat.

"Oh, Pinocchio," he cried in a tearful voice. "Give us a small gift of some kind, we beg of you! We are old, tired, and sick."

"Sick!" repeated the Cat.

"Farewell, false friends!" answered the Puppet. "You tricked me before, but you will never trick me again."

"Believe us! We really *are* poor and starving."

"Starving!" repeated the Cat.

"Farewell, false friends. Remember the old saying: 'Whoever steals his neighbor's shirt, usually dies without his own.' "

Waving good-bye to them, Pinocchio and Geppetto went on their way. They soon came to a tiny, straw cottage and knocked on the door.

"Who is it?" said a little voice.

"A poor father and a poorer son," answered the Puppet.

"Turn the key and the door will open," said the same little voice.

They went in. But they saw no one anywhere.

"Where is the owner of the cottage?" shouted Pinocchio.

"Here I am, up here!"

And there on a beam sat the Talking Cricket.

"Oh, my dear Cricket," said Pinocchio, bowing.

"Oh, now you call me your dear Cricket, but do you remember when you threw your hammer at me to kill me?"

"You are right, dear Cricket. Throw a hammer at me now. I deserve it! But do not hurt my poor old father."

"I am not going to hurt either of you. I only wanted to remind you of how you had once treated me. In this world of ours we must be kind to others, if we want to find kindness in our own days of trouble."

"You are right, little Cricket, and I shall remember the lesson you have taught me. But, tell me, how did you buy this pretty little cottage?"

"This cottage was given to me yesterday by a little Goat with blue hair. Then she went away crying, and it sounded to me as if she said: 'Poor Pinocchio, I shall never see him again. . . . The Whale must have eaten him by this time.' "

"Were those her real words? Then it was—it was—my dear little Fairy!" sobbed Pinocchio. After he had cried a long time, he wiped his eyes and made a bed of straw for old Geppetto. He laid him on it and said to the Talking Cricket:

"Tell me, little Cricket, where shall I find a glass of milk for my poor Father?"

"Farmer Giangio lives three fields from here. Go there and he will give you what you want."

Pinocchio ran all the way to Farmer Giangio's house and begged him for a glass of milk.

"A full glass costs a penny," said the Farmer.

"I have no penny," said Pinocchio sadly.

"Too bad, my Puppet. If you have no penny, I have no milk. But maybe we can make a deal. Do you know how to get water from a well?"

"I can try."

"Then go to that well over there and pull up one hundred bucketfuls of water. After you have finished, I shall give you a glass of sweet milk."

Pinocchio agreed to this and set to work. He had never worked so hard in his life.

"Until today," said Farmer Giangio, "my donkey has drawn the water for me, but now that poor animal is dying."

"Will you take me to see your donkey?"

"Gladly."

As soon as Pinocchio went into the stable, he spied a little donkey lying on a bed of straw—a donkey who looked familiar.

Pinocchio bent close and asked, "Who are you?"

The Donkey opened tired, dying eyes and answered, "I am Lampwick." Then he closed his eyes—never to open them again.

"Oh, my poor Lampwick," said Pinocchio, wiping away his tears.

"Why do you feel so sorry for a little donkey that you have just met?" asked the Farmer.

"Well, you see, he was once my friend." Pinocchio did not try to explain. He took his glass of milk and returned to his father.

For over five months, Pinocchio got up every morning and went to the farm to draw water. And every day he took a glass of milk for his poor old father, who grew stronger day by day. But he wanted to do even more. He learned to weave baskets. With the money he received for them, he bought food. He even built a wheelchair to take his father out into the air on bright, sunny days.

In the evening the Puppet studied by lamplight. He bought himself a book and taught himself to read and write. His work went along so well that he was able to save fifty pennies.

One day he said to his father, "I am going to the village to buy myself a coat, a cap, and a pair of shoes."

He ran out of the house, laughing and singing along the way. Suddenly he heard his name called, and noticed a large Snail crawling out of some bushes.

"Don't you remember me?" asked the Snail.

"I'm not sure."

"Do you remember the Snail that lived with the Fairy with Blue Hair, who opened the door for you one night and gave you something to eat?"

"Now I remember," cried Pinocchio. "Answer me quickly, pretty Snail, where is my good and kind Fairy? Has she forgiven me? Does she still love me? May I see her?"

"My dear Pinocchio, the Fairy is lying ill in a hospital. She has had much trouble, and she hasn't a penny left to buy a bite of bread."

"Oh! My poor, dear little Fairy! If I had a million dollars I would give it to her. But I have only these fifty pennies. I was just going to buy some clothes. Here, take them, little Snail, and give them to my good Fairy."

"What about the new clothes?"

"That does not matter. Go, and hurry. Come back here within a couple of days and I hope to have more money for you! Until today I have worked for my father. Now I shall also have to work for my mother. Good-bye, and please, for once in your life, hurry."

The Snail, surprising even herself, began to run as fast as a lizard in the hot sun.

When Pinocchio returned home, his father asked, "Where is the new suit?"

"I couldn't find one to fit me," said Pinocchio. "I shall have to look again some other day."

That night, Pinocchio worked two extra hours, and before falling asleep at midnight, made sixteen baskets instead of eight.

As he slept, he dreamed of his Fairy, beautiful, smiling, and happy, who kissed him and said to him, "Bravo, Pinocchio! In reward for your kind heart, I forgive you for all your old mischief. Boys who love and take good care of their parents when they are old and sick deserve praise. Keep on doing so well, and you will be happy."

At that very moment, Pinocchio awoke and opened wide his eyes.

To his surprise and joy he saw that he was no longer a Puppet. He had become a *real live boy*! He looked all around, and instead of the usual walls of straw, he found himself in the prettiest room he had ever seen. On a chair next to the bed, he saw a new suit, a new hat, and a pair of leather boots.

As soon as he was dressed, he put his hands in his pockets and found a little leather purse and note that read:

> *The Fairy with Blue Hair returns*
> *fifty pennies to her dear Pinocchio*
> *with many thanks for his kind heart.*

The Puppet opened the purse, and what do you think he found? Instead of fifty pennies, there were *fifty gold coins*!

Pinocchio ran to the mirror. He rubbed his eyes two or three times, wondering if he were asleep or awake, and decided he must be awake.

"And where is Father?" he cried suddenly. He ran into the next room, and there stood Geppetto, grown years younger overnight, bright and shiny in his new clothes and lively as could be. He was once more Mastro Geppetto, the woodcarver, hard at work on a lovely picture frame.

"Father, Father, what has happened?" cried Pinocchio, as he ran and hugged his father.

"This change in our house is all because of you, my dear Pinocchio," answered Geppetto.

"What have *I* done?"

"Just this. When bad boys become good and kind, they have the power of making their homes bright and new with happiness."

"And where is the old Pinocchio of wood?"

"There he is." Geppetto pointed to a large Puppet leaning against a chair, its head turned to one side, its arms limp, its legs twisted under him.

After a long, long look, Pinocchio said to himself with great peace and happiness:

"How foolish I was as a Puppet! And how happy I am, now that I have become a *real boy*!"

CARLO COLLODI

In 1826, Carlo Lorenzini was born to a cook and servant in Florence, Italy. As a child, he spent time in his mother's hometown of Collodi, which may be why he chose that for his pen name.

Although he briefly studied at a seminary, Carlo Collodi found writing and politics more interesting. He started several political magazines, wrote for newspapers, worked for the government, and even served in the army. After 1870, Carlo settled down and worked as a magazine editor. He translated a number of French fairy tales into Italian.

In 1881, Carlo Collodi sent a brief story about the adventures of a wooden puppet to a friend, who edited a newspaper in Rome. The friend published the first chapter of Pinocchio's story in *Giornale Dei Bambini* (*The Children's Journal*) in 1881. Pinocchio was a huge success in serial form. It soon became a book, which was first translated into English in 1892.

Carlo Collodi wrote other stories for children, but none as successful as *Pinocchio*. Collodi died in Florence on October 26, 1890.